Dear mouse friends,
Welcome to the world of

Geronimo Stilton

The Editorial Staff of
The Rodent's Gazette

1. Linda Thinslice
2. Sweetie Cheesetriangle
3. Ratella Redfur
4. Soya Mousehao
5. Cheesita de la Pampa
6. Coco Chocamouse
7. Mouseanna Mousetti
8. Patty Plumprat
9. Tina Spicytail
10. William Shortpaws
11. Valerie Vole
12. Trap Stilton
13. Dolly Fastpaws
14. Zeppola Zap
15. Merenguita Gingermouse
16. Shorty Tao
17. Baby Tao
18. Gigi Gogo
19. Teddy von Muffler
20. Thea Stilton
21. Erronea Misprint
22. Pinky Pick
23. Ya-ya O'Cheddar
24. Ratsy O'Shea
25. Geronimo Stilton
26. Benjamin Stilton
27. Briette Finerat
28. Raclette Finerat
29. Mousella MacMouser
30. Kreamy O'Cheddar
31. Blasco Tabasco
32. Toffie Sugarsweet
33. Tylerat Truemouse
34. Larry Keys
35. Michael Mouse

Geronimo Stilton
A learned and brainy
mouse; editor of
The Rodent's Gazette

Thea Stilton
Geronimo's sister and
special correspondent at
The Rodent's Gazette

Trap Stilton
An awful joker;
Geronimo's cousin and
owner of the store
Cheap Junk for Less

Benjamin Stilton
A sweet and loving
nine-year-old mouse;
Geronimo's favorite
nephew

Geronimo Stilton

A CHEESE-COLORED CAMPER

Scholastic Inc.

New York   Toronto   London   Auckland   Sydney

Mexico City   New Delhi   Hong Kong   Buenos Aires

No part of this publication may be reproduced, or stored in a retrieval system, or transmitted in any form or by any means, electronic, mechanical, photocopying, recording, or otherwise, without written permission of the publisher. For information regarding permission, write to Scholastic Inc., Attention: Permissions Department, 557 Broadway, New York, NY 10012.

ISBN 0-439-69139-7

Published by Scholastic Inc.
SCHOLASTIC and associated logos are trademarks and/or registered trademarks of Scholastic Inc.

Stilton is the name of a famous English cheese. It is a registered trademark of the Stilton Cheese Makers' Association. For more information, go to www.stiltoncheese.com.

Text by Geronimo Stilton
Original title: *Un camper color formaggio*
Cover by Larry Keys
Illustrations by Larry Keys and Topika Topraska
Graphics by Merenguita Gingermouse, Soya Mousehao, and
    Bafshiro Toposawa
Special thanks to Kathryn Cristaldi
Cover and interior design by Kay Petronio

12 11 10 9 8 7 6 5 4 3 2 1   5 6 7 8 9 10/0

Printed in the U.S.A.   08
First printing, February 2005

MR. STILTON, WAIT!

One morning, I was in a f**a**bum**o**use mood. I woke up before my alarm clock went off.

I made myself a delicious cheesy good breakfast. And I got a seat on the subway. Not an easy thing to do in crowded New Mouse City!

I was humming a happy tune when I reached my office.

Just then, my secretary came racing up to me. "Mr. Stilton, wait!" she squeaked. "Don't open that door!"

But I had already turned the knob. How strange. Someone was sitting at my desk.

GRANDFATHER WILLIAM SHORTPAWS

He was a large mouse with silver fur and shiny steel glasses. He was holding **my** phone in one paw. The other paw flipped through **my** desk calendar. He looked so comfortable in **my** chair, you'd think he owned the place. And, well, he did.

You see, the mouse was **my** grandfather. **GRANDFATHER WILLIAM SHORTPAWS.** He was the founder of the company.

Oops. I completely forgot to introduce myself. My name is *Stilton, Geronimo Stilton*. I am a publisher. I run

the most popular newspaper in New Mouse City. It's called the *The Rodent's Gazette.*

But where was I? Oh, yes, I was staring at my grandfather. "Hello, Grandfather," I squeaked. "How are you?"

THREE, I SAID THREEEEE!

"HOW DO YOU THINK?" roared Grandfather William. **"I'M BUSY! VERY BUSY, THAT'S HOW I AM!"**

I gulped. Can you believe I am afraid of my own grandfather? But I don't let it get to me. You see, everyone is afraid of Grandfather William. He is one tough, no-nonsense mouse. Once he made a ten-pound rat cry just by glaring at him.

Now he was *SCREAMING* into my phone. I felt sorry for the poor mouse on the other end.

"Yes, three!" he shrieked. "I need 3 million guidebooks to Ratzikistan on the double! I said, Three! Three! *Threeee!*

Grandfather William Shortpaws

T as in **Try harder!**
H as in **Hop to it!**
R as in **Right away!**
E as in **Exactly what I said!**
E as in **End of discussion!**"

He snickered. Then he slammed down the phone.

I chewed my whiskers. "**Um**, what are you doing here, Grandfather?" I asked in a faint voice. "And why do you want to print three million guidebooks to Ratzikistan?"

As usual, Grandfather ignored me. He is the worst listener. Instead, he began scribbling away on **my** notepad.

Just then, **my** secretary, Mousella MacMouser, came in. She handed Grandfather a stack of papers. He leafed through them, grumbling. "**These are all wrong!**" he snorted. "Wrong, wrong, wrong!" He tore up the

papers and crumpled them into a ball. Then he JUMPED onto **my** desk. He struck a pose just like a professional **basketball** mouse. *"SCORE!"* he squeaked, shooting the ball into my wastepaper basket.

My secretary and I looked at each other in shock.

"The business is a mess, Geronimo!" he snorted. "You need to publish some bestsellers now or you can say bye-bye to your books forever!"

I had no idea what Granddad was squeaking about. The company was doing GREAT. The newspaper was selling like cheese Popsicles in the summertime. And our books always sold well. Yes, we hadn't had a bestseller in a few months, but we were still making **tons** of money.

Of course, Grandfather William wouldn't listen. "Don't tell **me** how we're doing!" he shrieked. "**I** built this company with my bare paws! I know everything!"

Uh-oh. This was going to be a lot harder than I thought.

Once Grandfather gets an idea in his head, it sticks like a mouse in a glue trap. He's like the safe at the Regal Rodent Bank. A tough one to crack.

I tried reasoning with him. "Um, but, Grandfather," I began in a gentle voice. "**20** years ago, you left running the company to me. Isn't this my job?"

Can you guess his reply? Naturally, he didn't say a *word*. I told you my grandfather never listens.

He was staring at my calendar. "Look at

all these appointments!" he squeaked. "I'm going to be busier than a ratburglar in the middle of a blackout."

"But, Grandfather!" I complained. "Those are **my** appointments!"

At that very moment, the phone rang. We both leaped for it. Unfortunately, the old mouse **beat** me to it.

"No, this is not Geronimo Stilton," he thundered. "I am his grandfather. And from today on, I am the one in charge.

The head honcho.

The boss. The big cheese.

Got it?" He slammed down the phone.

I was horrified. What would my clients think? Maybe Grandfather was right. The business was a **mess**. And it was all because of him!

NOT EVEN PENGUINS . . .

Right then, I remembered about the guidebooks. "Grandfather, can you at least tell me about these guidebooks to Ratzikistan?" I asked. "I just don't *understand*."

Grandfather William shook his head. "Poor Geronimo," he scoffed. "Of course you don't understand. Can you help it if your brain is so small? So teeny-weeny? So microscopic? Not everyone can be a genius like me."

By now, I was ready to STRANGLE him. But how could I? I could just see the headlines in the paper the next day: YOUNG PUBLISHER MURDERS FEEBLE OLD GRANDFATHER! STILTON SNUFFS OUT INNOCENT LIFE! No, I couldn't do it. After all, I'm a newspaper mouse. I hate bad press.

Instead, I tried again. "Are you really going to print three million copies?" I asked.

For once, Grandfather William seemed to hear me. He rolled his eyes. "Wake up, Geronimo! Wake up! *WAKE UUUUUUP!*" he shouted in my ear. Then he *WAVED* a map under my snout.

"What's that?" I mumbled, taken by surprise.

He sneered and shoved the map at me again. This time I could see it clearly. It was a map of Ratzikistan.

"Have you ever noticed that there are no guidebooks to Ratzikistan?" Grandfather **demanded**.

I opened my mouth to reply, but he was already babbling on.

"Ah, Ratzikistan," Grandfather said with

a *sigh*. "A place no one has ever heard of before. Just think of all of the guidebooks we can sell!" He clapped his paws. "Sometimes I am so smart, I scare myself!" he chuckled.

I was stunned. Had Grandfather William's cheese finally slipped off his cracker? No one goes to Ratzikistan. Not even penguins.

"But, Grandfather," I began. "There are no guidebooks to Ratzikistan because the temperature there is *forty degrees below zero!*"

MY SWEET LITTLE CHEESE CURL!

Suddenly, the office door flew open. In marched my sister, **Thea**. She is *The Rodent's Gazette*'s Special correSpondent. Have you met her? You would remember Thea. She's one of a kind. Kind of a nut, that is.

"Grandpa, dear Grandpa!" my sister squeaked. She threw herself into Grandfather's open paws.

Immediately, his eyes filled with tears. "Thea, my beloved granddaughter! My sweet little **cheese curl**! More precious than my wallet! More beautiful than Miss Mouse Island!" he cried.

Thea smiled **sweetly**. "See your

sister, here, Geronimo?" my grandfather added **proudly**. "Now, this is one smart rodent!"

Can you tell Thea is Grandfather William's favorite? He sends her on all of these wonderful assignments. In fact, **SHE HAD JUST RETURNED FROM A TRIP TO THE SOUTHERN ISLANDS.** She was researching the latest trends in swimwear. Tough job, I'm sure.

"Well, it seems this year it's all about **color**!" Thea announced.

"**Orange, red, yellow, green!** You name it, they're wearing it!"

Grandfather beamed. "Brilliant! I'm so proud of you, darling!" he gushed.

I tried not to act jealous. But I was. I cleared my throat. "Um, I would love to go to the Southern Islands sometime, too," I offered **timidly**.

Grandfather William shot me a **disapproving** look. "***Forget it***, Geronimo," he squeaked. "Only a stunning mouse like Thea can report on fashion. She's ***got style***. Too bad I can't say the same about you."

I chewed my whiskers to keep from squeaking. What was wrong with the way I dressed? OK, so maybe I was a little on the conservative side. I wasn't into *flashy* colors or *crazy* prints. But no one had ever picked on my clothes before.

Grandfather turned to *Thea*. "How was the flight, darling?" he asked. "I hope your first-class seat was comfortable. Nothing but the best for my little *treasure*."

Did I mention Thea is Grandfather's favorite?

Thea's got style.

TINA SPICYTAIL

Right then, the phone **rang**. I pressed the speaker **BUTTON** so we could all listen.

"Heeeeello! Heeeeeellooooo!"

squeaked the female voice at the other end. I recognized it right away. It was **Tina Spicytail**, Grandfather's housekeeper.

"*Mr*. Geronimo, would you please ask *Mr*. Shortpaws what he would like for dinner?" she yelled. Tina was not a quiet mouse.

Grandfather William scratched his head. "Let's see, I'd like a cheddar fondue . . . " he began.

But Tina quickly interrupted him. "No fondue for you, *Mr*. Shortpaws!" she

shrieked. "You're on a diet! By the way, are you wearing your woolen underwear? You're not so young anymore, you know! Don't come crying to me if you catch a **TERRIBLE COLD!**"

Grandfather rolled his eyes. He started to reply, but she cut him off again.

"Before I forget, I'm packing your suitcases for your trip," she announced. "I must have packed forty at least. I had a little trouble with your antique desk, though. But don't worry, I just chopped it up into **pieces**. You can put it together when you arrive at your destination."

Steam poured out of Grandfather William's ears. His eyes popped open wide.

"**WHAT?!**" he thundered. "Do you mean **YOU CHOPPED UP MY PRECIOUS ANTIQUE DESK** with the imported ivory knobs?"

Uh-oh. I had a feeling Grandfather wasn't going to like the answer to that question.

"**YOU GOT IT!**" Tina confirmed proudly. She went on to explain that she had also included his favorite armchair. It was chopped into pieces like the desk. "I am all ready to leave. I will be there in a couple of minutes!" she finished.

YOU CHOPPED UP MY PRECIOUS ANTIQUE DESK?!

A dial tone filled the room. And an alarm bell **went off** inside my head. Grandfather was leaving? Where to? And why?

Just then, he turned to me. "Better get packing, Geronimo," he said. "You know how slow you are. You don't want to make us late."

I had no idea what he was talking about. **I wasn't planning on going anywhere.**

Grandfather William shook his head. "Oops, didn't we tell you?" he said.

Thea raised her eyebrows. "Oops, didn't we tell you?" she echoed.

Right then, my cousin Trap strode into the room. He was wearing a huge backpack. **"OOPS, DIDN'T WE TELL YOU?"** he squeaked.

The door flew open again. This time, Tina marched in. She was pushing an

enormouse trunk on wheels. She looked at everyone staring at me.

"Didn't you tell him?" she shouted.

I bit my tail in a fit of **RAGE**. "Tell me what? What didn't you tell me?" I screamed.

At that moment, my favorite nephew, Benjamin, raced through the door and **hugged** me.

"Uncle Geronimo! I am so **happy**!" he cried. "They just told me that you are coming with us to

Ratzikistan!"

*My favorite nephew, Benjamin, raced
through the door and hugged me.*

RATZIKISTAN, HERE WE COME!

I was flabbergasted. "what? We are leaving for Ratzikistan? Why didn't anyone tell me?" I shouted.

No one squeaked. What could they say? They knew they were wrong.

Instead, Thea shoved a chocolate Cheesy Chew into my mouth. "Don't get your tail in a twist," she soothed in a honey-sweet voice.

I was still fuming. But I must admit, I do love those Cheesy Chews. There's nothing like a yummy piece of chocolate to PERK me up. Still, I wasn't giving in so easily. I was tired of being overlooked. "I will not be ignored!" I spluttered with my mouth full.

Trap **rolled his eyes**. "You're such a drama queen, Germeister," he chuckled. He glanced at his watch. "Better shake a paw, Cuz. You have exactly seventeen and a half minutes to pull yourself together, pack your suitcases, and put on the alarm system before we're off!" he added. Then he pinched my cheek, causing the Cheesy Chew to go down the wrong pipe.

"**Argh! Argh!**" I gagged.

Grandfather clapped a paw on my back. The candy flew across the room.

"My dear grandson, quit complaining. We'd never ignore you!" he insisted. "Now stop **dillydallying** and close your suitcases."

I gnashed my teeth together. I took a deep breath. Then I explained in a very small voice why I couldn't close my suitcases. I didn't have any!

"Even better!" Grandfather William concluded. "Then you can leave without them! Let's go! Call a **TAXI**!"

By now, I was beyond mad. I was a raging ball of fur. I dug my paws into the carpet.

"I'm not leaving! And you can't make me!"

I squeaked. Yes, I sounded just like a five-year-old mouslet. But I didn't care.

Grandfather William **STARED** at me for a moment. Then he told everyone to leave the room.

"I need to be alone with my dear grandson," he exclaimed.

As soon as they left, Granddad slumped against me. Then he li**mp**ed over to my chair. *Since when did he have a limp?* I wondered.

"Ah, Grandson, getting old is such a horrible thing. You are so lucky to be young and strong," he said in a feeble voice.

I blinked. I had never thought about Grandfather William being old before. He was so loud. And tough. And, well, obnoxious.

"Are you OK, Granddad?" I asked, feeling guilty.

He shook his head. "I'm not feeling well. I have a pain right here, near my heart," he said, pointing at his breast pocket.

I raised my eyebrows. "But, Grandfather,

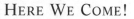

that's your wallet," I pointed out.

He shrugged. "Ah, yes. My heart, my wallet, same thing," he added.

I wasn't surprised. Grandfather loves money more than *cheese*. He's the cheapest mouse I know. He once shaved off all of his fur to save money on shampoo and conditioner. That's why they call him Cheap Mouse Willy.

Now he stroked his fur, looking sad. "It kills me to see our family arguing," he mumbled. "I am so hurt that *you* don't want to come with *us*."

He *sighed*. Then his eyes filled with tears.

I didn't know what to say. I didn't want to leave. But I had never seen Grandfather so broken up.

"Say you are coming with us, *dear grandson*!" he cried, grabbing my paw.

"Please say yes! Do it for me. I have given you **SO MUCH** and I ask for so little."

By now, he was sobbing away full force. I had never seen so many tears come out of one rodent before. He would have come in handy when my aunt Sweetfur's mouse hole went up in flames.

At last, I couldn't stand his sobs any longer. "OK, OK. I'll come," I muttered.

At that very moment, the unthinkable happened. Grandfather William leaped back to his feet. It was a miracle! It was as if he were suddenly thirty years younger.

"Well, then, let's hit the road!" he shrieked. "The taxi is here!"

He flung open the office door. Thea, Trap, and Benjamin fell on top of one another. Their ears had been pressed to the door.

"Wait, **Grandfather**!" I called.

But he was already halfway down the hall. "Move your tail, *you spineless fool*!" he shouted back at me.

Let's hit the road!

GRANDFATHER'S SUPERCAMPER

I couldn't believe it. My own grandfather had set me up. I thought he really *was* sick. Even worse, I thought he was heartsick. Now I knew he was just nuts. Nuts enough to pull a low-down prank on me.

Rotten rats' breath! I was in a sour mood. Anyone who knows me knows that **I HATE TRAVELING!**

My grandfather, on the other hand, was **bursting** with excitement.

"Isn't traveling great?" he squeaked happily. "In my next life, I think I will be an **explorer**. I will soar above the clouds in my own private jet. Sail the high seas in my yacht. And, of course, I will hit the road in my

fabumouse cheese-colored camper."

LET'S GO!

I **sighed**. Grandfather wasn't dreaming about the camper. He really does have a cheese-colored camper. He putters along in the fast lane at **20** miles per hour, annoying all of the other drivers. They **flash** their headlights at him. They honk their horns. But there's no budging Granddad. He's like a snail on a superhighway.

Actually, Grandfather doesn't drive a camper. He drives a *supercamper*. It's longer than fifty mice standing tail to tail.

It's painted a deep cheddar **yellow**. And it's filled with everything you can imagine.

Kitchen **Dining Room** **Bathroom**

The driver's cabin has a **SATELLITE NAVIGATIONAL** system. It lets you pinpoint your position anywhere around the world.

An enormous **crystal** chandelier hangs in the camper's dining room. This is where Grandfather William

Bedroom

Grandfather's Office

likes to eat Tina's five-course gourmet meals. Grandfather's bedroom has a four-poster bed and its own marble bathroom. There's even a *yellow* Jacuzzi shaped like a slice of cheese!

Besides all of that, there are a couple of guest rooms, an elegant library filled with old books, and a room just for luggage. The place is **bigger** than my entire mouse hole!

Oh, and I didn't even tell you about the kitchen. It's a cook's dream. It has a real stone oven. And a COMPUTERIZED giant REFRIGERATOR. It tells you when supplies are getting low. Tina loves it. Of course, she travels with Grandfather wherever he goes. Yep, Tina and her silver extendable rolling pin. She never leaves home without it. It was

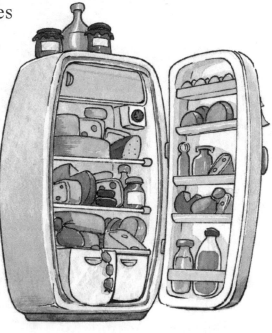

a gift from Granddad. At night, she keeps the rolling pin within paw's reach for protection. Once she accidentally knocked

Tina Spicytail

Grandfather William over the head with it. She thought he was a ratburglar!

Still, Tina does a lot more than just cook. In fact, she's one multitalented rodent. She can give an INJECTION and fix a flat tire without twitching a whisker. And even more important, Tina keeps Grandfather in line. She's the only rodent I know who is not afraid of him. As I said, she's one **tough mouse**!

KING OF THE ROAD

At last, we were ready to leave. Granddad drove down the block. Two minutes later, we discovered we had a little problem. No, make that two little problems. Benjamin and Trap had come down with rodent pox! They were covered from head to paw with

RED BUMPS. We returned home to drop them off.

Now there were only four of us. Granddad, of course, sat behind the wheel. Tina **banged** pots and pans in the kitchen. My sister took pictures, leaning out the window. And I read the map. I tried to give Grandfather William directions, but as usual, he wouldn't listen. When I told him to turn left, he insisted on turning right.

"Don't be a **BACKSEAT DRIVER**, Grandson!" he barked. "I know where we're going. You forget, I've **TRAVELED** all over the world. I have my own map right here inside the old noggin." He tapped his head. "Yep, I've got a memory like a steel trap. I can find my way to the Swiss Cheese Islands with my eyes closed. I can make it to Mouse Everest with

one paw tied behind my back. I can even walk and **chew cheese** at the same time."

In the end, we got lost.

We traveled for hours along a deserted road. We didn't pass one **SINGLE** road sign.

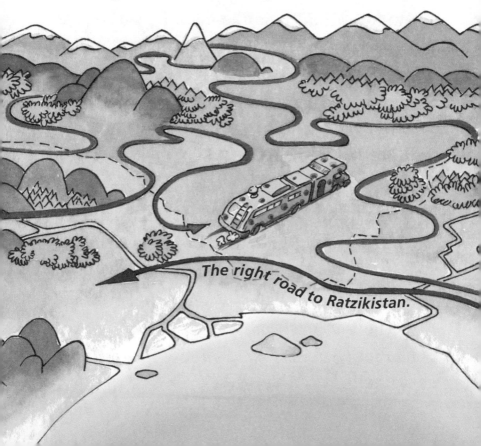

The right road to Ratzikistan.

By nightfall, we found ourselves in the **MIDDLE** of a forest. Granddad didn't seem to mind. He just kept driving and driving.

I tried to use the super-high-tech **SATELLITE SYSTEM**. But it was so confusing. And the instruction manual was missing. **Finally**, Grandfather pulled over. "I think I'll take a rest," he announced. "Who wants to drive?"

No one **SQUEAKED**. Do you want to know why? It's an absolute nightmare driving with Granddad. He barks out orders the whole time. He even throws a fit if you blink! Grandfather William says he is **king of the road**. Sometimes he even wears a crown while he's driving. It was a gag gift from Trap. But Granddad took it seriously.

"Who's taking the wheel? No time for dillydallying!" Grandfather shouted now. "I can't do it all! Even a genius needs to rest sometimes."

GERONIMO, DO SOMETHING!

We were all in a panic. We couldn't keep driving. We were terribly lost.

"Geronimo, *do something*!" Thea whispered to me. "Maybe you can go out and look for help."

I *turned pale*. Me? Go out into the deep, **DARK** woods? I'd rather cut off my tail. Well, OK, maybe not my tail. Maybe my whiskers. Or maybe just some fur.

"Wh-wh-why m-m-m-me?" I stammered.

My sister gave me a look. "Oh, stop being such a scaredy mouse, Geronimoid," she scolded. "I'd go *myself* but I haven't showered. What if I ran into a cute mouse?"

I rolled my eyes. My sister goes on more

dates than Sylvia Sizzlefur, the famouse movie star.

Just then, Tina winked at my sister. She waved her rolling pin at me. "*Mr.* Stilton, would you mind going outside for a minute to SEE if it is raining?" she asked.

I had barely left the cabin when . . .

SLAM!

The door shut behind me. I heard the lock click.

Cheese niblets! I had been tricked again.

I screamed for them to let me in, but no one answered.

I was all alone.
In the dark, spooky woods!

I heard my sister singing in the shower. She'd probably be in there for an hour—and then spend another hour fluffing

Was she making a double-cheese lasagna?

her fur! It was as if she'd forgotten about me! Didn't she care about me at all?

Tina was back in the kitchen. I could hear her rolling pin slamming the countertop.

What was she making this time? A double-cheese lasagna? A cheddar casserole?

I SObbed. I would never get a chance to find out. I just knew something horrible was going to happen. I mean, I was in the middle of the **wilderness**. And it was so dark.

What if a **WILD ANIMAL** attacked me? What if I fell off an icy cliff?

What if space mice picked me up and brought me back to their leader?

Oh, how could my sister do this to me? She's the one who's not afraid of anything. She is the bravest mouse I know. Nothing scares her. She loves:

1. parachuting off dangerous mountaintops

2. racing her motorcycle

3. practicing karate (she's a black belt)

4. doing stunts with her airplane

5. extreme survival camps

Yes, my sister, Thea, is one courageous mouse. She's not afraid of *anything or anyone*. What a show-off.

I looked around, shivering. The forest was as **black** as ink. Luckily, I remembered I had a tiny flashlight attached to my key ring. I pulled it out. The *light* was faint.

Are you afraid of the dark? I am!

SHADOWS loomed everywhere. The branches on the trees looked like skeletons reaching for the sky. Moths transformed into *bats*. A bird screeched overhead. I gulped. My paws shook so hard, I almost dropped the flashlight.

Then I saw a shadow. It was behind me.

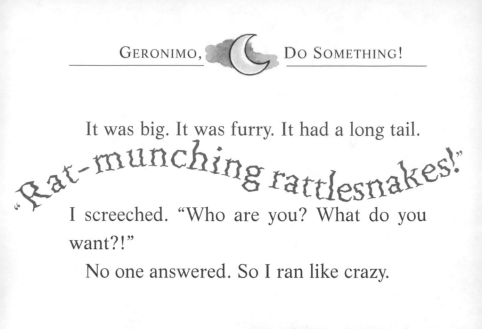

It was big. It was furry. It had a long tail.

"Rat-munching rattlesnakes!"

I screeched. "Who are you? What do you want?!"

No one answered. So I ran like crazy.

The shadow followed. I tripped. The shadow tripped, too. I got up. The shadow got up, too.

Just then, it hit me. I was running from my own shadow!

STILTON HIMSELF?

I stopped. I wanted to go back to the camper. But now I had no idea where I was. I started running down a path. It had to lead somewhere, right?

I RAN AND RAN AND RAN . . . until I tripped again. Did I mention I'm a bit of a klutz? My snout banged into the **ground**. Youch!

I sat up in a daze. That's when I saw him. A furry rodent staring down at me.

"Grandfather?" I mumbled. "How did you find me? Where's the camper?"

The other rodent flashed a blinding light in my eyes. "Grandfather?" he repeated. He sounded confused.

I STOOD UP. No, this wasn't my cranky granddad. It was a **STRANGER**. He had a big square head, a square snout, and square shoulders. Even his tail looked square. How odd.

"Who are you? What do you want?" he squeaked warily.

I told him my whole tale. About Grandfather William, the supercamper, and getting lost. I left out the part about me running from my shadow. I didn't want him to make fun of me. After all, we had just met.

Then I told him my name, *Geronimo Stilton*.

"Stilton!" he exclaimed. "*Geronimo Stilton*, the famouse writer? I have read all of your books!" He shook my paw, excitedly. "My name is Sylvester Squaretail," he

announced. "May I have your autograph? With my name, too?"

I grinned. I must admit I love running into my fans. They're so sweet. So sincere. So smart. How do I know they're smart? They must be. They like to read my books!

I didn't have any paper, so I wrote my autograph on a leaf. I hoped Sylvester didn't drop it in the woods. He'd never find it in this dark, creepy place.

DOUBLE-CHEESE LASAGNA

Sylvester slipped the leaf into his pocket. I could tell he was one happy rodent.

I chewed my whiskers. I'd be happy, too, if I could find my way back to the camper. And what about Ratzikistan? Maybe Sylvester knew how to get there.

"**Ratzikistan!**" he exclaimed when I asked. "You're in the middle of the Fossil Forest. Ratzikistan is in the **OPPOSITE** direction."

Cheese niblets! I knew Grandfather had been driving the wrong way. I groaned.

"Don't worry," said Sylvester. "I can tell you how to get back to your camper. Then I'll give you directions to Ratzikistan."

It took him half an hour to explain everything. There was a lot to remember. I thought about writing everything down on some leaves. But I didn't want to rip up ten bushes. I love nature too much.

Sylvester shook my paw and said goodbye. "Have a safe trip!" he called, heading off.

I started down the path. As I walked, I mumbled the directions.

"Let's see, I take the path for ten minutes until I reach the BEECH TREE," I began. "Or was it an OAK TREE? Then I turn right two or three times and cross the brook. At the brook, I head upstream, or maybe downstream. Then I come to a boulder shaped like a cat's head. Or was it a rat's head? Then I cross a small bridge and turn LEFT, then RIGHT.

No, maybe it was RIGHT, then LEFT . . ."

I tramped through the woods for more than an hour. **RATS!** I was lost again. Oh, why didn't I write those directions down? So what if I destroyed a few bushes? So what if there were fewer leaves in the world? Was that such a crime?

I sat down on a rock. Tears sprang to my eyes. "How did I get myself into such a mess?" I sobbed. "It's late and I'm hungry. I should be home in *my cozy mouse hole*. I should be nibbling on a triple-decker grilled-cheese-and-tomato SANDWICH right now."

Just then, I sniffed the air. Was I dreaming? Did I really SMELL CHEESE?

I sniffed again. Yes, I was sure of it. It was the scent of a double-cheese lasagna!

I pulled myself together and got back on

the path. I followed the heavenly scent. Before long, I spotted the twinkling lights of the camper.

I squeaked with joy. Home at last!

I couldn't wait to tell my family about my adventures. They would be so happy to see me. They must have been worried sick when I didn't RETURN.

Inside, I found them all seated at the table.

Thea glanced up. "Oh, it's just Geronimo."

"Who?" asked Grandfather.

"Geronimo!" Thea repeated.

Grandfather William shoved more lasagna into his mouth. "Oh, did he go out?" he muttered.

I sank onto the sofa. I told them how I got lost. Then I explained about the lasagna. "I

followed the scent back to the camper," I said.

Tina smiled. She was very proud of her cooking. Especially her double-cheese lasagna.

"Speaking of lasagna," I continued. "Can you cut me a piece?"

Now Tina was practically glowing. "Nope, it's all gone!" she announced triumphantly. She held up the empty pan. "*Your grandfather* even licked the pan clean. So much for his diet," she added.

My stomach **RUMBLED** in protest. I couldn't believe my family hadn't saved a single piece of Tina's delicious lasagna for me! I was starving after my midnight ramble through the forest.

Oh, why had **I come** *on this* **miserable trip?**

FIVE POUNDS OF CHEDDAR

The next day, we left at dawn. I pointed Grandfather in the right direction.

For once, he listened to me. What a **SHOCK**. Maybe he was feeling sick. I didn't ask. I was just happy to be moving again.

"Oh, *I'm a traveling mouse! Whoa! Whoa! Whoa!* I'm a traveling mouse!" Grandfather William sang.

I **groan**ed. Granddad's singing sounded like the shrieks of a mouse with his tail caught in a trap.

We **drove** farther and farther north.

The landscape began to change. Instead of green trees and bushes, there were snow - covered valleys. Icy mountains dotted the horizon. I noticed that the sunlight was getting dimmer and dimmer. It seemed we had left fall behind and headed straight into winter. And it wasn't just any old winter. It was the coldest winter on the planet.

At lunch, we stopped for a break. I put on my thermal underwear. I put on my heavy parka. I put on my cat-fur hood. But nothing kept the cold out. The air froze my whiskers. I had to defrost them back in the camper.

We drove on and on. Weeks went by. Finally, one day, a road sign EMERGED through the fog.

R-A-T-Z-I-K-I-S-T-A-N

"Ratzikistan! Cheese niblets, I did it! We're here!" Grandfather William exclaimed. He pulled over.

"I must find a supermarket immediately," Tina declared.

I stared out into the fog. "Something tells me there aren't any supermarkets in Ratzikistan," I told her. "In case you haven't noticed, we're in the middle of nowhere!"

Tina snorted. She grabbed her canvas shopping bag (no paper bags for Tina). Then she jumped out of the camper. She looked around. Then she began hiking

Ratzikistan

toward a **dir ty** *little* shop on the corner.

Rotting fruit and piles of smelly fish filled the shopwindow. Inside, there were crates and boxes everywhere. What a dump. I peered into one of the CRATES. It was filled with jelly jars. I picked one up. Little white balls of something floated in a MURKY LIQUID. They looked just like eyeballs. I gulped.

An army of ants crawled out the side of another box. Each ant carried a piece of SMELLY green cheese. My stomach lurched.

Ears of shriveled corn on the cob stuck out of a wicker basket. I pulled one out and shrieked. It was covered with tiny worms! By now, I was feeling faint. Did I tell you I'm afraid of ants? Did I tell you I'm afraid of worms? Did I tell you I'm not too crazy about electric toothbrushes, either? Oh, but that's another story. . . .

I watched as Tina marched up to the rodent behind the counter. He had a crooked tail and a crooked smile. She pulled out a long shopping list. "I'll need five pounds of your best cheddar! Six jars of your finest **sardines**! And three loaves of your freshest *SEVEN-GRAIN BREAD*!" she barked.

The rodent dropped his crooked smile. His **EYES** opened wide. Still, he didn't say a word. After all, what could he say? It was clear they didn't have those things in this

store. "Forget it, Tina," I whispered. "I told you this is not a regular supermarket. THERE ARE NO SUPERMARKETS IN RATZIKISTAN."

Tina stamped her paw. One thing you should know about Grandfather's housekeeper. She never takes no for an answer. And I mean **never**. Once a waiter told Tina that she could not meet the chef at her favorite Italian restaurant, Squeakolini's. She threw a fit. First she threw her napkin in the air. Then

she threw her spaghetti in the air. Then she threw her waiter in the air.

"I will not forget it," Tina insisted. She slapped her shopping list on the counter. "Give this to your boss," she told Crooked Tail.

He disappeared into the ᑲᗇᏨ of the shop. A few minutes later, another rodent came out. He was carrying all the things Tina had asked for.

Tina shot me a smug look. **"No supermarkets, my paw!"** she smirked.

A Cast-iron Stomach

We climbed back into the camper. Tina put away the food. Soon Grandfather revved up the engine and we were off again.

I stared out the window as we drove along. Icy streams flowed down from the tops of gigantic glaciers. Snowcapped mountains dotted the landscape.

Thea snapped away with her camera. "This place is like a winter wonderland," she remarked.

We drove on into the night. The road grew steeper. We crossed over a narrow bridge. We climbed along a rugged gorge.

Patches of ice covered the road. I broke out in **A COLD SWEAT**. One slip and we'd all be goners. We'd be nothing but a camper full of **CAT FOOD**. I felt faint. Oh, why had I come to Ratzikistan? It was one big mountain mess. And I was afraid of heights!

At last, we reached a clearing. It overlooked all of the valleys below.

Grandfather pulled over. He jumped out of the camper, clapping his paws. "Now, this is what I call good clean air!" he squeaked, taking a deep breath. "Someone write this down. We need to tell tourists to stop *at this very spot*. The view is more breathtaking than the inside of the Cheesy Chews factory!"

My sister began typing away on her laptop. She had been taking notes the whole trip to put in our guidebook to Ratzikistan.

"What would I do without my darling granddaughter?" Granddad William beamed. Then he scowled in my direction.

"It's a shame you're not more like your sister, Geronimo," he added. "It's a wonder you two are related!"

I decided to take a walk. My tail was **flat** from sitting in the camper for so long. Plus, I needed to stretch my paws a little. Get the old blood pumping. Get away from Granddad.

I took a few steps, but I didn't get far. Seconds later, Tina's whistle practically pierced my eardrums. She  uses it to signal that dinner is ready.

"Come on, shake a paw!" she called. "You don't want your food to get cold!"

We sat down at the table. Tina was busy dishing up the meal. She placed one OLIVE and a piece of lettuce on Grandfather William's plate. Recently, she had decided he needed to go back on his diet.

Granddad stared at his plate and sighed.

"No complaining," Tina scolded. "You need to drop those pounds or we'll have to roll you home!"

Then she turned her attention to me. Uh-oh. Tina had **other plans for me**. Recently, she had decided that I was too thin. She began piling my plate high with food. I watched in horror as she filled an enormouse bowl to the brim with spaghetti. Then she slapped down plate after plate of pies, casseroles, puddings, breads, and more. There was no way I could eat all of that food. It was enough for ten mice, not one!

I felt sick. "Um, but, Tina," I began. "I have a weak stomach. I don't think —"

"**NONSENSE**!" Tina interrupted me. "I'll **fix** that stomach of yours. You just need to fill it with a ton of food. Soon you'll be able to eat stones!"

I **CRINGED**. But I didn't tell Tina I wasn't interested in eating stones. I didn't want her to hit the roof.

Meanwhile, Grandfather was eyeing my *food* with envy. He tried to steal a roll, but Tina slapped his paw away.

"I'm doing this for your own good!" she told Granddad. "As for you, *Mr.* Geronimo, you need to try **harder!**"

I opened my mouth to complain. Bad idea. Tina picked up a spoon and ***STUFFED*** my mouth *full of lard*.

"See, that wasn't so bad, was it?" she chuckled.

I couldn't answer. Have you ever tasted *lard*? Think glue, only ten times worse!

THE SUN HAS BEEN KIDNAPPED!

That night, I had horrible dreams. First I was drowning in a vat of creamy butter and lard. Then I was being chased by a ten-foot ham-and-cheese sandwich waving a pickle.

I **WOKE UP** with a start.

I **STARED** out my window. It was **dark**.

Was it still the middle of the night? No, my alarm clock said it was ten in the morning.

My fur stood on end. I woke up my sister.

"Thea! **The sun has been kidnapped!**"

I squeaked.

Not Me!

My sister looked at the **DARK SKY**. She picked up her globe. She punched in some numbers on her calculator. She pawed through her atlas. The whole time, she was mumbling something about longitude and latitude. Finally, she sat back and sighed. "Now I know why it is still dark," she said. "Ratzikistan is so far north, there are only a few *hours* of daylight here."

We started driving again.

The dark sky made me depressed. Who would buy a guidebook on a place where the sun never shines?

Oh, why did I come on this **MISERABLE** trip? I could be home warming my fur in the bright sunshine. I could be sipping a mozzarella milk shake at Happypaw's Outdoor Café. I could be planting yellow flowers in my garden. Well, OK, I didn't actually have a garden. But I always wanted one.

I was **still** dreaming about home when I realized something was wrong. We weren't moving. What was Granddad doing? Stopping for another scenic view? It would be hard to see much in the dark.

"Well, that's it," Grandfather William announced. "We're out of gas."

He took out a

big can from under his seat.

Then he waved it under my snout.

"SOMEONE needs to find a gas station," he squeaked, staring right at me.

I chewed my whiskers.

"Who's going to go?" I asked suspiciously.

"*Not me, I'm too old*," grumbled Grandfather.

"*Not me, I'm a lady*," squeaked Thea.

"Not me, I'm cooking!" shouted Tina. "I'm making pizza."

I stared out the window. There was no way I was going out there. It was dark. The ground was **FROZEN**. There were no **TREES OR BUSHES** or happy woodland animals. We were miles away from civilization. Not my kind of place. I like lots of rodents. I like taxis. I like bright lights. Oh, how I missed New Mouse City!

Two seconds later, Granddad pushed me out the door.

Why does he never listen to me?

"Don't worry, Mr. Geronimo!" Tina called after me. "I'll keep a nice slice of pizza **WARM** for you!"

I left the camper. I had no choice. They had locked the door behind me!

COULD IT BE SANTA MOUSE?

Right then, I heard the sound of jingling bells. A mouse was coming toward me. He was riding a sled pulled by reindeer.

I BLINKED. What was SANTA MOUSE doing in Ratzikistan? Christmas was already over.

I took a closer look. No, it wasn't Santa. It was just a local rodent on a **sled**.

"Slow down, please!" I shouted. "I need a ride!"

But he didn't seem to understand. I waved my gas can in the air. "I need gas!" I tried.

He just smiled and **ZIPPED** right by me.

I began running after him. My heart was pounding. My muscles ached. Sweat poured down my fur. If only I spoke Ratzikistani. Oh, where was a good translator when you needed one?

Suddenly, I spotted something up ahead. Could it be? Yes, it was. A little bus stop stood on a hill.

I gathered all of my strength and sprinted for it.

Cheesecake! Somehow I got there before the sled. I held up my paw for him to stop.

This time he got it. **"STOP?"** he asked.

I nodded. I was so exhausted, I couldn't even squeak.

I pulled myself onto the sled. We took off at *BREAKNECK* speed.

CRAZY RIDER

CHEESE NIBLETS! Sled Mouse was a **crazy** driver. He was going so fast, it felt like we were flying. I held on for dear life. We plunged down steep slopes. We rocketed over **frozen** lakes. I squeezed my eyes shut. Oh, when would this miserable ride be over?

Sled Mouse didn't seem to notice I was shaking like a leaf. He kept chattering away. Of course, I had no idea what he was saying. Maybe it was better that way. I might have been even more terrified. I wasn't sure this rodent had all his marbles. He kept doing wacky things like dropping the reins to blow his nose. Or **SCRATCH** his whiskers. Or eat a breath mint.

Sled Mouse was a crazy driver.

Each time the sled went into a slide, I began to squeak. "**WATCH** the road, I mean the snow, I mean be careful!" I cried.

Each time, he would burst out laughing. Did I say something funny? I wasn't trying to be funny. I was just trying to stay alive!

Why, oh, why had I climbed onto this sled? I could have walked. I had two paws. So it might have taken me a little longer to get somewhere. So what? At least I wouldn't end up FLATTENED in a sled crash. I could just see the headlines now: STILTON SQUISHED TO SMITHEREENS IN SLED ACCIDENT! PUBLISHER SLIDES OFF THE FACE OF THE EARTH!

I shivered. What a way to go. What a **NIGHTMARE**. What a strange glowing light in the distance! Could it be a gas station? I blinked back tears. **Holey cheese!** It was! I stopped myself from breaking into a song and dance. I didn't want to set off the madmouse at the reins.

He screeched to a stop in front of the pump. I POPPED OUT OF THE SLED as fast as my quivering paws could take me. "Thank you!" I squeaked.

Sled Mouse grinned. Then he took off. I must say, I wasn't entirely sad to see him go.

But now I had a new **PROBLEM**. How would I get back to the camper? I filled up my can with gas and paid the attendant.

The attendant introduced me to a mouse who was filling up his snowmobile. He offered me a ride. Before getting on, I asked him a few questions. "You're a safe driver, right?" I said. "You don't go **FAST**, right?"

He laughed as if to say, *"I'm the safest driver on the planet."* Then he said something in Ratzikistani and gave me a **crash helmet**.

Uh-oh. I wasn't feeling good about this. But what choice did I have? I had to get back to the camper. Oh, why had I left it in the first place?

With a **SIGH**, I climbed onto the snowmobile. We took off like a pair of schoolmice on the first day of summer **VACATION**.

HEEELP! HOW DO YOU RIDE THIS THING?

I COULDN'T BELIEVE IT. It was happening all over again. I was off on another wild ride. *Were all Ratzikistanis this crazy?* I wondered. *Or did I just get lucky?* Rancid rat hairs! It couldn't get any worse than this.

COULD IT?

Half an hour later, it did. The crazy mouse driver started **squeaking** at me in Ratzikistani. For some reason, he kept pointing to the handlebars. What was he trying to tell me? I didn't have a clue. Maybe he was just showing me the parts of the snowmobile. I decided to play along. "Yes, the handlebars are for steering." I nodded. What next? The wheels? The horn? Did snowmobiles even have horns? I didn't know. I had never been on one before.

Just then, the driver **SLAPPED** me on the back. He pointed to the handlebars again. Then he fell sound asleep. I tried waking him up. But it was no use.

"**Help!**" I **shrieked** in a panic. "How do you ride this thing?"

My cry rang out in the darkness. Of course, no one answered. What nutty rodent would be outside on such a freezing cold night? Or was it day? Who knew? It seemed like it was always nighttime in Ratzikistan. Oh, how I hated this horrible, **dark** place.

Suddenly, I realized we were **RACING** down an incredibly steep hill. "No!" I screamed. "I want to get off! I want to go home! **I want my mommy!**"

Next to me, I could hear my driver happily

Heeelp!

snoring away. Then the snowmobile hit the ground. It was a miracle. We were all still in *ONE PIECE*.

Finally, my driver woke up. He STRETCHED. He YAWNED. Was this mouse for real? *Couldn't he see we were speeding along out of control? Couldn't he see I was about to have a nervous breakdown?*

Right then, a big cheese-colored shape appeared before my eyes. It was the camper!

flash! flash! flash!

Flashes of light snapped in the darkness. My sister, Thea, was taking pictures. Rats! My fur must look like a mess. But there was no time to worry about it now. "Where are the brakes?!" I shrieked in a panic.

At last, the driver took over. He spun around right in front of the camper. I was _thrown out_ of the snowmobile. I landed snout-first in an enormouse snowbank.

The driver tossed me the gas can. Then he **SPED OFF.**

My sister took one last picture of me with a snout full of icicles. "These pictures are perfect for our book!"  she declared. "And I've got the perfect caption: Fun times in Ratzikistan!"

I didn't have the **strength** to reply.

I dragged myself to the camper. **Could it get any worse?** I wondered.

And then it did. As soon as I walked in,

Tina stuffed a **SIZZLING** slice of pizza into my mouth. Have you ever burned your tongue on hot pizza? I **HOWLED** in pain.

"See, *Mr.* Geronimo, I told you I'd keep your pizza warm," Tina said proudly.

Why, oh, why had I come on such a crazy adventure?

I'm Not a
Sportsmouse

We spent the next few days r◎aming ar◎und Ratzikistan. We tried to interview the locals. But it was hard. After all, they didn't speak English. We couldn't understand one **SQUEAK**.

Then my sister decided one of us should try all of the local **SPORTS**. Guess who was the lucky mouse? That's right, yours truly.

Oh, why does my family like to torture me? They know I'm not a sportsmouse. I'm always the last rodent picked for a team. Still, there I was, joining in on a . . .

A. snowball fight (They creamed me two seconds after I made my first snowball.)

B. contest for the best-built snowmouse (I accidentally knocked the **HEAD** off when I tried to put on whiskers.)

C. mountain hike (They carried me back on a stretcher.)

D. **skating race** (I fell through a crack in the **ICE**. When they pulled me out, I was **FROZEN** solid.)

E. stinky fish contest (I lost. But I'm telling you, mine was the stinkiest.)

F. **class on how to build an igloo** (My door was so small, I was trapped inside.)

HEAVENLY CHEDDARELLA!

We were all feeling depressed.

It was clear Ratzikistan wasn't exactly a great vacation spot. "Who would want a guidebook to this place?" my sister said with a sigh. I shrugged. What could I say? Who would want to visit a place that was forty degrees below zero? A place where the sun never shines? A place where all the fish are stinky?

Thea switched off her LAPTOP COMPUTER. It was time to go home. For once, even Grandfather William agreed.

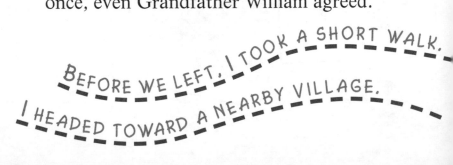

BEFORE WE LEFT, I TOOK A SHORT WALK. I HEADED TOWARD A NEARBY VILLAGE.

I passed a house. Through the window, I saw a Ratzikistani family having dinner. They were happily munching on a very tasty-looking golden-yellow cheese.

Right then, one of the mice saw me at the window. She invited me in. I tried to say no, but she didn't understand. She pulled me inside. Immediately, I was hit with the most amazing scent. It was coming from the golden-yellow cheese. The mouse cut me a slice. This time, I didn't refuse. I took a nibble. Then two. Then three. CHEESECAKE! It was the best cheese I had ever tasted in my life! It was more delicious than the chunkiest cheddar. It was more tasty than the best blue cheese. I

was in heaven. I had to find out the name of that cheese.

"What do you call this?" I asked the mouse who had invited me in. She grinned. Then she said, *"CHEDDARELLA."*

I shook my head. Was she making fun of me? It sounded like she'd said "cheddar," but it didn't taste like any cheddar I'd ever eaten.

"No," I tried again. "The name. Can you please tell me the name of this cheese?"

"CHEDDARELLA," she repeated in a louder voice.

Now I didn't know if she meant cheddar or mozzarella. Oh, why do mice like to tease me? Do I look like a pushover?

"Please, madam," I insisted. "I don't have time for jokes. I just want to know the name of this cheese."

I saw a Ratzikistani family having dinner.

This time she pounded the table. She picked up the cheese and held it under my snout. *"CHEDDARELLA! CHEDDARELLA! C-H-E-D-D-A-R-E-L-L-A!"* she squeaked at the top of her lungs.

I slapped my forehead. Now I got it. It was called cheddarella cheese. Who would have thought such a **scrumptious** cheese would have such a funny name?

I ran to tell the others.

DON'T LOOK SO WORRIED . . .

Thea was the most excited about the golden-yellow cheese. "I have the most brilliant **IDEA!**" she squeaked. That **night**, I heard her typing away on her computer. What was my crazy sister up to now?

You just never knew with Thea. One time, she tried to get into the fashion business. She began *designing her own clothes*. She made me test out all of her samples. I was running around in **skirts** for weeks. Everyone at the office made fun of me. Lucky for

me, Thea came to her senses. She realized she was better at shopping for clothes than making them.

The next morning, Thea scampered into the kitchen. In one paw she held a cup of steaming coffee. In the other was a wad of papers. "Here it is!" she announced. "The ANSWER to our GUIDEBOOK PROBLEM!"

I chewed my whiskers nervously. What had Thea cooked up this time? There was no way she'd get me in a dress again. And I put my paw down at the thought of high heels.

"Don't look so worried, Gerry Berry," my sister giggled. "My idea is really very simple."

And it was. No mouse would want to buy a

guidebook on Ratzikistan, Thea reminded us. But every mouse would love to sink his or her teeth into some delicious cheddarella cheese.

"Instead of a guidebook, we'll publish a cookbook!" Thea squeaked. "We can fill it with yummy cheddarella cheese recipes!"

DELICIOUS CHEDDARELLA

OUR COZY HOME

We had all kinds of adventures on our way home.

One day, we got stuck in the middle of the woods. A tree had FALLEN in front of our camper. To get through, we had to SAW IT into small PIECES. Can you guess who did all of the sawing? You guessed it! I had blisters all over my paws!

After that, we had a flat tire. We were trying to avoid a caribou.

Later on, we got caught in a SNOWSTORM. We were snowed in for three days.

Tina kept our spirits up with her delicious cheddarella cheese dishes. Plus, I must admit it was **nice** to be together. I was getting used to our cozy four-wheeled home.

ONE THING
AT A TIME

I sat next to Grandfather on the way home. I had to give it to the old mouse. He never seemed to get tired. He was **STUCK** to the wheel from dawn till dusk. He never spoke while driving. "When I am driving, I concentrate on the road," he explained. "The secret of success, Geromino, is to do just one thing at a time!"

I thought about what Granddad had said. I watched the road unfolding before us. It was pretty fascinating. At each turn, we saw something different.

Maybe traveling wasn't so bad after all, I decided. Still, I couldn't wait to get back to my comfy mouse hole. I'd slip my paws into my **CAT-FUR** slippers. I'd whip up a tasty mozzarella milk shake. I mean, don't get me wrong, Grandfather William's supercamper was awesome. But I love my *home sweet home*.

"You look tired, Geronimo," Granddad observed. "Why don't you get some rest? I'll be fine."

I SMILED. Yes, Grandfather could be obnoxious at times. He was one rodent who really knew how to drive me up a clock. But he really wasn't such a bad mouse.

He had lots of crazy ideas, sure, but some of them were good ones. And I knew that no matter what, he *loved* me.

ANOTHER DAY, ANOTHER ADVENTURE

When I woke up, I spotted a **sign** on the side of the *road*. Cheese niblets! We were almost home!

Grandfather let me **drive** the rest of the way. Of course, he had to scream a few commands from the backseat. "Not too fast! **Not too slow!** Stop on red! Go on green!" he called.

Welcome to
New Mouse
City

I didn't even care. We were going home.

At last, we reached New Mouse City. Rodents rushed along the sidewalks.

Taxicabs screeched and honked their horns. Buildings

touched the sky. Ah, *beautiful New Mouse City*. Have you ever been there? There's really no place like it!

Even though I was thrilled to be home, I felt *sad* leaving everyone. I was used to Tina's yummy meals. (Although I could do without the force-feeding.) And Granddad had grown on me.

"The best way to get to know a rodent is to travel with him," Granddad always said. I guess he was right. I knew a lot about Grandfather after this trip.

I climbed out in front of my house. Thea called a taxi. Grandfather William and Tina boarded the camper again.

"Will I see you tomorrow, Grandfather?" I asked.

He chuckled. "Who knows, Geronimo," he replied. "Tomorrow is another day.

Another day, another **adventure**!"

Tina **waved** good-bye with her silver rolling pin. Then they both vanished into the night.

JUST GRANDDAD

Would you like to know how it all ended? Well, let me tell you. Our cookbook, *Secret Recipes from Ratzikistan*, was a huge success. **Three** million copies were sold!

Yesterday I got an e-mail from Grandfather. "See? I told you so! Three million copies! Three! Three! **Threee**!!!!" he wrote.

Did I mention that Grandfather loves it when he's right?

I have stopped saying that *I hate traveling*. I mean, how else can you see the world? I am even planning a Christmas trip with the family!

Yes, Thea and Trap will pick on me.

Tina will make me eat **TONS** of food.
And Granddad, well, he'll just be Granddad.
*But I guess that's not such a bad
thing after all. . . .*

ABOUT THE AUTHOR

Born in New Mouse City, Mouse Island, Geronimo Stilton is Rattus Emeritus of Mousomorphic Literature and of Neo-Ratonic Comparative Philosophy. For the past twenty years, he has been running *The Rodent's Gazette*, New Mouse City's most widely read daily newspaper.

Stilton was awarded the Ratitzer Prize for his scoop on *The Curse of the Cheese Pyramid*. He has also received the Andersen 2000 Prize for Personality of the Year. One of his best-sellers won the 2002 eBook Award for world's best ratlings' electronic book. His works have been published all over the globe.

In his spare time, Mr. Stilton collects antique cheese rinds and plays golf. But what he most enjoys is telling stories to his nephew Benjamin.

Want to read my next adventure?
It's sure to be a fur-raising experience!

WATCH YOUR WHISKERS, STILTON!

Cheesecake! A mysterious one-eyed rat was
trying to steal *The Rodent's Gazette* from
under my snout! There was only one mouse
who could save the paper—Shif T. Paws,
my crafty former business manager. Shif
booked me onto the infamouse TV game
show *The Mousetrap*. If I won, *The
Rodent's Gazette* would be saved. But if I
lost—SQUEAK!—those scary TV rats
would chop off my tail!

Don't miss any of my other fabumouse adventures!

#1 Lost Treasure of the Emerald Eye

#2 The Curse of the Cheese Pyramid

#3 Cat and Mouse in a Haunted House

#4 I'm Too Fond of My Fur!

#5 Four Mice Deep in the Jungle

#6 Paws Off, Cheddarface!

#7 Red Pizzas for a Blue Count

#8 Attack of the Bandit Cats

#9 A Fabumouse Vacation for Geronimo

#10 All Because of a Cup of Coffee

#11 It's Halloween, You 'Fraidy Mouse!

#12 Merry Christmas, Geronimo!

#13 The Phantom of the Subway

#14 The Temple of the Ruby of Fire

#15 The Mona Mousa Code

#17 Watch Your Whiskers, Stilton!

and coming soon

Geronimo's Joke Contest

Do you like telling your friends jokes that make them squeak? So do I! And I'm always looking for new jokes. Send me a few of your favorites, and I'll send you a fun gift. If you make me laugh out loud, your joke may appear in one of my future bestsellers!

Send your **JOKE** along with your name, mailing address, city, state, zip code, and birthday to me at the following address:

Thundering Cattails, I Want to Make Geronimo Stilton Laugh Out Loud!
c/o Scholastic Inc.
557 Broadway
Box 711
New York, NY 10012

THE RODENT'S GAZETTE

1. Main Entrance
2. Printing presses (where the books and newspaper are printed)
3. Accounts department
4. Editorial room (where the editors, illustrators, and designers work)
5. Geronimo Stilton's office
6. Storage space for Geronimo's books

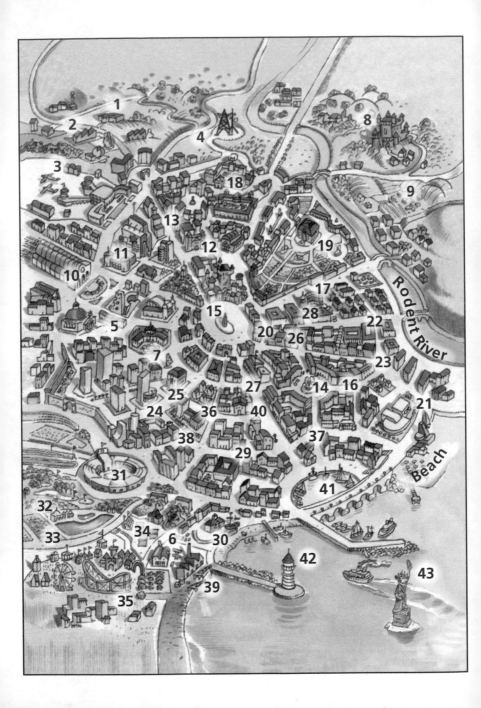

Map of New Mouse City

1. Industrial Zone
2. Cheese Factories
3. Angorat International Airport
4. WRAT Radio and Television Station
5. Cheese Market
6. Fish Market
7. Town Hall
8. Snotnose Castle
9. The Seven Hills of Mouse Island
10. Mouse Central Station
11. Trade Center
12. Movie Theater
13. Gym
14. Catnegie Hall
15. Singing Stone Plaza
16. The Gouda Theater
17. Grand Hotel
18. Mouse General Hospital
19. Botanical Gardens
20. Cheap Junk for Less (Trap's store)
21. Parking Lot
22. Mouseum of Modern Art
23. University and Library
24. *The Daily Rat*
25. *The Rodent's Gazette*
26. Trap's House
27. Fashion District
28. The Mouse House Restaurant
29. Environmental Protection Center
30. Harbor Office
31. Mousidon Square Garden
32. Golf Course
33. Swimming Pool
34. Blushing Meadow Tennis Courts
35. Curlyfur Island Amusement Park
36. Geronimo's House
37. New Mouse City Historic District
38. Public Library
39. Shipyard
40. Thea's House
41. New Mouse Harbor
42. Luna Lighthouse
43. The Statue of Liberty

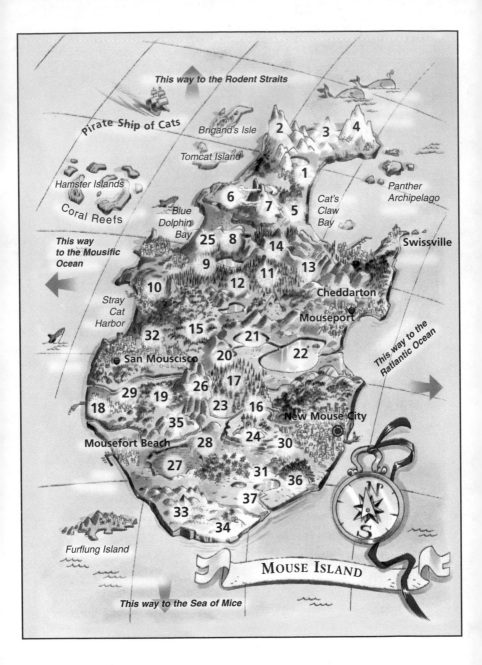